Dear Parents and Educators,

Welcome to Penguin Young Readers! As parents and educators, you know that each child develops at his or her own pace—in terms of speech, critical thinking, and, of course, reading. Penguin Young Readers recognizes this fact. As a result, each Penguin Young Readers book is assigned a traditional easy-to-read level (1–4) as well as a Guided Reading Level (A–P). Both of these systems will help you choose the right book for your child. Please refer to the back of each book for specific leveling information. Penguin Young Readers features esteemed authors and illustrators, stories about favorite characters, fascinating nonfiction, and more!

That Bad, Bad Cat!

LEVEL 2

GUIDED READING LEVEL **E**

This book is perfect for a **Progressing Reader** who:
- can figure out unknown words by using picture and context clues;
- can recognize beginning, middle, and ending sounds;
- can make and confirm predictions about what will happen in the text; and
- can distinguish between fiction and nonfiction.

Here are some **activities** you can do during and after reading this book:
- Picture Clues: Use the pictures in this book to tell the story. Have the child go through the book, retelling the story just by looking at the pictures.
- Make Connections: Ask the child if he/she has had a pet that has misbehaved. What did he/she do in that situation? If the child hasn't been in this situation yet, ask what he/she would do if his/her pet misbehaved.
- Make Predictions: At the end of the story, the cat becomes "that good, bad cat!" Ask the child what he/she thinks the good, bad cat will do next.

Remember, sharing the love of reading with a child is the best gift you can give!

—Bonnie Bader, EdM
Penguin Young Readers program

*Penguin Young Readers are leveled by independent reviewers applying the standards developed by Irene Fountas and Gay Su Pinnell in *Matching Books to Readers: Using Leveled Books in Guided Reading*, Heinemann, 1999.

For Mary and her very good cat, Fiona—CM

For Eloise and Charlotte Lindblom—TK

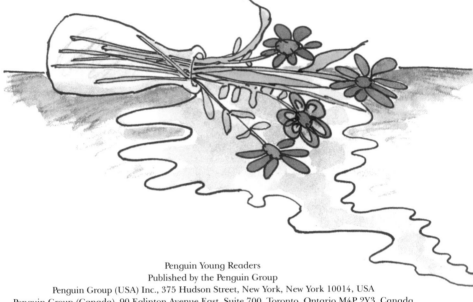

Penguin Young Readers
Published by the Penguin Group
Penguin Group (USA) Inc., 375 Hudson Street, New York, New York 10014, USA
Penguin Group (Canada), 90 Eglinton Avenue East, Suite 700, Toronto, Ontario M4P 2Y3, Canada
(a division of Pearson Penguin Canada Inc.)
Penguin Books Ltd., 80 Strand, London WC2R 0RL, England
Penguin Group Ireland, 25 St. Stephen's Green, Dublin 2, Ireland (a division of Penguin Books Ltd.)
Penguin Group (Australia), 250 Camberwell Road, Camberwell, Victoria 3124, Australia
(a division of Pearson Australia Group Pty. Ltd.)
Penguin Books India Pvt. Ltd., 11 Community Centre, Panchsheel Park, New Delhi—110 017, India
Penguin Group (NZ), 67 Apollo Drive, Rosedale, Auckland 0632, New Zealand
(a division of Pearson New Zealand Ltd.)
Penguin Books (South Africa) (Pty.) Ltd., 24 Sturdee Avenue,
Rosebank, Johannesburg 2196, South Africa

Penguin Books Ltd., Registered Offices: 80 Strand, London WC2R 0RL, England

Text copyright © 2002 by Claire Masurel. Illustrations copyright © 2002 by True Kelley. All rights
reserved. First published in 2002 by Grosset & Dunlap, an imprint of Penguin Group (USA) Inc.
Published in 2011 by Penguin Young Readers, an imprint of Penguin Group (USA) Inc.,
345 Hudson Street, New York, New York 10014. Manufactured in China.

Library of Congress Control Number: 2002280493

ISBN 978-0-448-42622-8   10 9 8 7 6 5 4 3 2 1

That Bad, Bad Cat!

by Claire Masurel
illustrated by True Kelley

Penguin Young Readers
An Imprint of Penguin Group (USA) Inc.

Once there was a cat.

The cat scratched the table.

The cat scratched the chair.

"Bad, bad cat!"

his family said.

He tore up the pillows.

He tore up the bed.

"Bad, bad cat!"

his family said.

He ate the plants.

He pulled up the flowers.

"Bad, bad cat!"

his family said.

He spilled milk.

He stole food.

"Bad, bad cat!"

his family said.

One day, the cat ran outside.

"Do not go far!"

his family said.

But he did.

He was not back for lunch.

"That bad, bad cat,"

his family said.

He was not back for dinner.

Now his family began to worry.

"Kitty! Darling! Sweetie! Honey!"

they called.

"Please come back!"

They looked all over for him.

They asked everybody,

"Have you seen our cat?"

Without him,

the house was not the same.

"I miss him."

"I miss him."

"We miss him."

Every day they left treats.

And they left a window open,

just in case.

And he did come back!

They hugged him.

They kissed him.

"You are a good, good cat.

Don't ever run away again!"

He loved them,

no matter what they said.

And they loved him . . .

no matter what he did—

that good, bad cat!